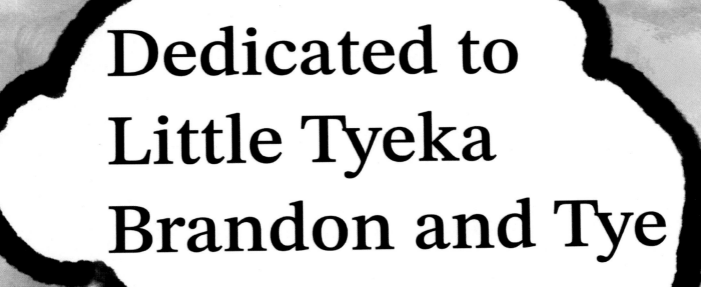

Dedicated to
Little Tyeka
Brandon and Tye

I
Love
You

Always
Believe
In you!

Sleeping peacefully, Tye arose
as the smell of pancakes filled her nose.

She jumped out of bed as the sun shined on her face.
She shouted, "I wonder what I'll do today!"

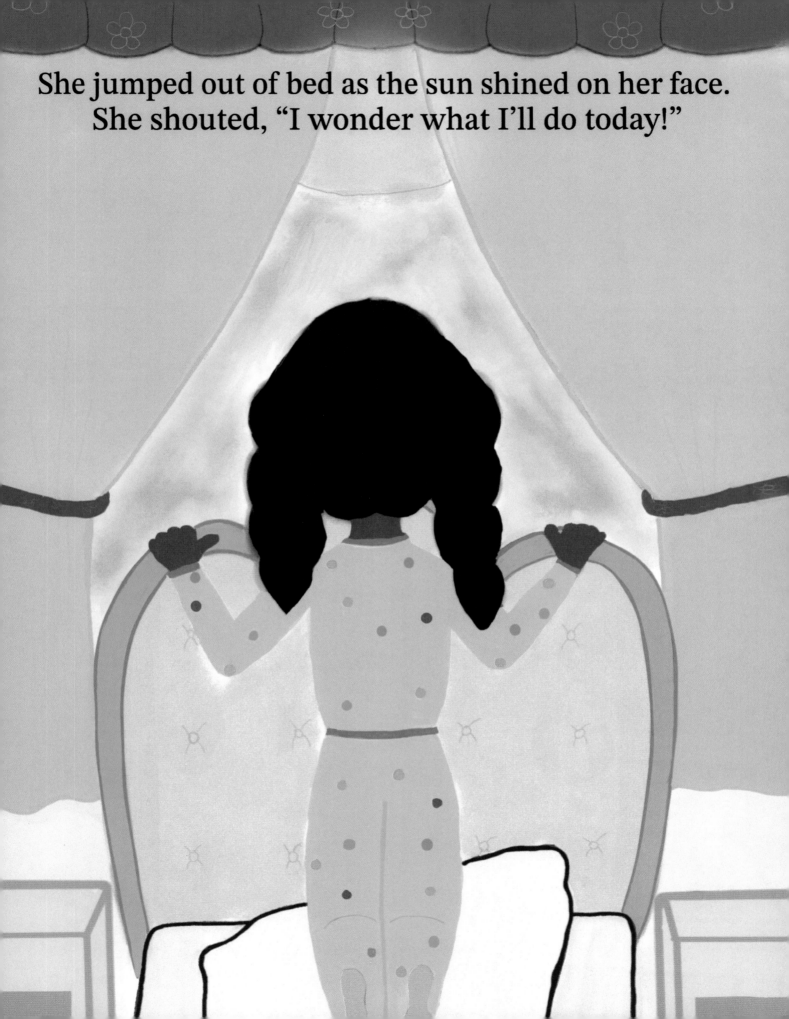

Where should I go? Who should I be?
I'll bake chocolate chip cookies, or climb a tree.

Tye put on her favorite shirt then started to prance.
She wiggled and jiggled and put on her pants.

The old, torn, blue jeans, that fit ever so snug.
She put on her socks with a push and a tug.

She picked up her shoes and put them on her long feet.

Tye hopped to the bathroom to brush her teeth.

She pondered and pondered as she brushed away.
I wonder what I'll do today.

I could fly a plane tye thought, as she brushed her hair.

"I could sail a ship", Tye said heading down the stairs.

"Oh I know!" Tye exclaimed as she stuffed her face.
I'll call up London! We'll have a race!

Tye finished her apple juice then headed out,
when mom asked, "what is all the fuss about?"

Tye turned around and started to sigh,
"I don't know what to do today" Tye replied.

Mom said "there are so many things you could do, the sun is out, take a dip in the pool.

Tye thought to herself that's a great idea. I'll call up Katie and kattalia.
We can play in the pool, then jump rope right after
Excitedly, Tye called her friends, but there was no answer .

Tye plopped on the couch and turned on the TV.
She flipped through the channels, then feel fast asleep.

Awake from her nap, Tye saw princess Markel.
On TV in a dress that glittered and sparkled.

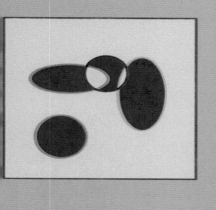

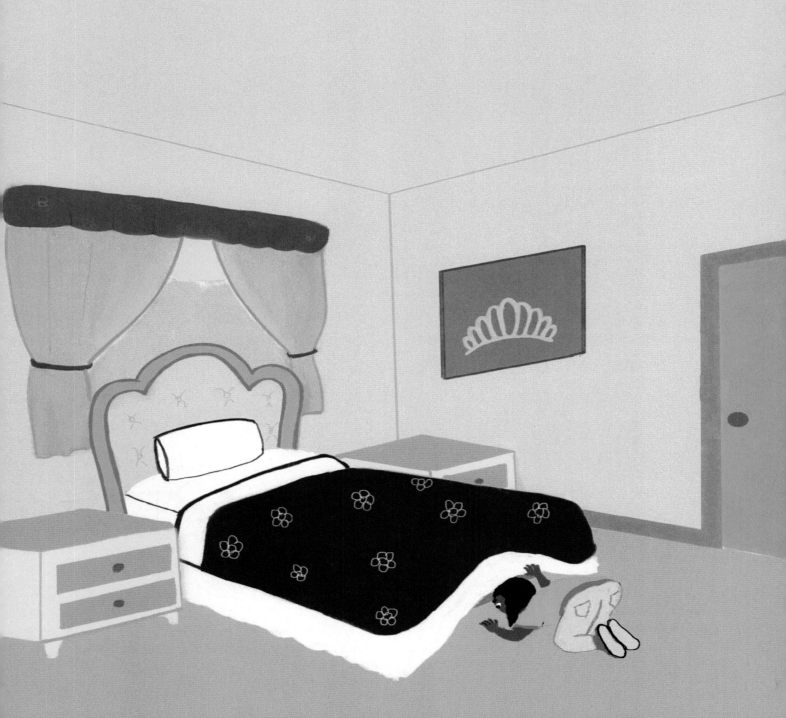

Suddenly a lightbulb appeared over Tye's head,
then she ran up the stairs and looked under her bed.

She pulled out a box as she wore a big smile.
She emptied the box on the floor in a pile.

She picked up a tiara with a twinkle in her eye, and said "I know what to do, I'll be princess Tye!"